CLARA
ROUNDS CAPE HORN

CLARA ROUNDS

CAPE HORN

BY

GAIL FABER and MICHELE LASAGNA

MAGPIE PUBLICATIONS • ALAMO, CALIFORNIA

Acknowledgements

The authors would like to thank the following persons for their generous contributions of time and effort.

Frances Bowles, Editor

Florence Cahill, Word processing

William Kooiman, J. Porter Shaw Maritime Library, Fort Mason, San Francisco, CA

Brenda Markson, Spanish teacher, language consultant

Sharon Marocchi, Fourth grade teacher, editing

Ann-Marie Soldavini, Computer layout, California Concepts Design & Type, San Leandro, CA

First Edition May 1997

Published by Magpie Publications
Box 636
Alamo, CA 94507

ISBN: 0-936480-12-2 Student soft cover edition
ISBN: 0-936480-13-0 Student hard cover edition
ISBN: 0-936480-14-9 Teacher edition

To the real Clara

Clara's Voyage
From Boston to Monterey
1845

Dear Reader,

In the early 1840s there were only two ways to travel from the east coast of the United States to California . . . overland by covered wagon following the rough trails made by fur trappers, or sailing by ship around Cape Horn, the most southerly tip of South America. The people who came to California in these early years were a part of the beginning of the Westward Movement.

The sailing ships that came to the sleepy ports of California before the Gold Rush were called square-riggers because of their large square sails. The deep holds of these ships were stacked high with cargo to be traded for hides and tallow from the vast California ranchos.

Here begins the story of nine year old Clara Frances Allen. Clara and her parents are ready to board a heavily loaded trading ship bound for Monterey, California.

Leaving the harbor of Boston, Clara watches as the captain gives orders to the crew. The sailors push the heavy bars that turn the capstan and haul up the two thousand pound anchor. Other sailors heave on the lines and hoist the sails. Clara soon learns that these hard-working sailors work day and night to keep the ship in good shape and on course.

As Clara begins the fifteen-thousand mile, four month ocean journey, she finds that she is the only child on board. Before long, Clara makes friends with the entire crew of the *Lady Shellhorn* . . . including Mrs. Captain, Asa, the cabin boy, Mr. Simon, the sailmaker, Mr. Turk, the carpenter, and Sam-Lee, the cook.

In her daily journal, Clara writes her experiences, thoughts, and feelings. Read along with her as she writes about the people she meets, the ocean animals she sees, and the yarns she hears. From wild storms to the boring days of the Doldrums, Clara's story makes each of us feel that we, too, are a part of this exciting square-rigger adventure.

Have a good journey as you go round Cape Horn!

The Authors

Outward Bound

"Oh for a fair and gentle wind,"
    I heard a fair one cry;
But give to me the roaring breeze,
    And white waves beating high;
And white waves beating high, my boys,
    The good ship tight and free,
The world of waters is our own,
    And merry men are we.

Jacob Faithful

Table of Contents

Chapter One   *A Time for Good-Byes* 1

Chapter Two   *Aboard Ship* 5

Chapter Three   *Our Home at Sea* 13

Chapter Four   *"Haul Away, Joe"* 17
                     A Sea Shanty 18

Chapter Five   *Tour of the Ship* 23

Chapter Six   *My Friend, Asa* 29

Chapter Seven   *Sam-Lee* 35

Chapter Eight   *Rio de Janeiro* 43

Chapter Nine   *Mr. Simon, The Sailmaker* 47

Chapter Ten   *Child Overboard* 51

Chapter Eleven   *Where is Murphy?* 57

Chapter Twelve   *Carmen's Trunk* 61

Chapter Thirteen   *Blackbeard the Parrot* 65
                     The Story of Blackbeard the Pirate 66

Chapter Fourteen   *Penguins Don't Fly* 69

Chapter Fifteen   *Rounding Cape Horn* 73

Chapter Sixteen   *The Doldrums* 77

Chapter Seventeen   *Monkey Business* 83

Chapter Eighteen   *A Little Excitement!* 87

Chapter Nineteen   Good-Bye to the Doldrums 91

Chapter Twenty   Below Decks 93

Chapter Twenty-One California at Last! 99

Bibliography 105

Glossary 107

As you read **Clara Rounds Cape Horn** you will notice words that you may not know. These words are listed and defined for you in the glossary at the back of this book.

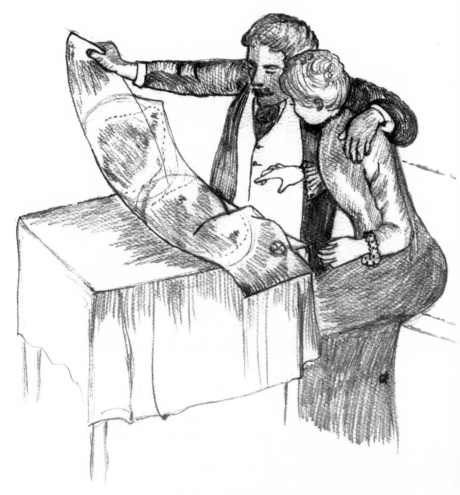

*Mother and Father spent many hours planning
our sea voyage to California.*

Chapter One

A Time For Good-Byes

August 10, 1845
Leaving Boston

It was August 10, 1845, the day we were leaving Boston. I felt as if a heavy weight were sitting on my shoulders. I had never seen my bedroom look so bare. My dresser stood empty. On my bookshelf, the books that I couldn't take with me leaned sadly to one side. Nails on the wall showed where my favorite pictures had hung.

I folded the last of my clothing into the small boot trunk that my mother had given me for our sea journey. As I closed and locked the lid on my trunk, I heard myself sigh.

I'd miss my bed with the big feather mattress. I'd miss the rocking chair that my father had made for me. I'd miss the seashells that I had collected along the beach at Cape Cod. Most of all I'd miss Callie, my cat, and her five kittens who were already living downstairs with our landlady, Mrs. Murphy.

I sat on the edge of my bed and stared down at my shiny new black shoes. I noticed that one of my shoes was scuffed. It must have happened when I had crawled under my bed to get my journal. I put my hand deep into my skirt pocket and felt the smooth leather of my journal. I could also feel the raised letters on my journal that spelled my name, Clara Frances Allen. My journal is one thing I would not want to leave behind. As I sat on my bed, I could see myself in the mirror that hung on the wall. I pushed back the curly brown hair that fell around my face. Mother had tied it back with a ribbon, but as usual my hair never stayed in place. I stood up and slowly put on the new red coat that father had bought me for this journey. As I buttoned my coat, I glanced out the window at the chilly early morning fog.

In the next room I could hear my mother, Elsie, and my father, Pearlie, talking as they finished packing their trunks. I heard them mention a familiar name . . . Uncle Frank. Ever since my Uncle Frank had gone to California, my parents had talked about joining him. My uncle had written long letters to us in Boston telling us about his life in California. My parents had read the letters over and over again. His letters were like stories about a make-believe land far away. Uncle Frank told about his rancho and the herds of cattle he

2

owned. He told us about his wife Maria and his twin sons Pablo and Hector. He told us about his favorite horse, Dorado, a golden-colored horse with a black mane and a black tail.

Not long ago, my parents had asked me if I would like to see Uncle Frank again. When I asked if Uncle Frank had come home, they told me that we were going to California! Uncle Frank needed my father, Pearlie, to help him manage his large rancho. My mother and my father said that we would be leaving soon on a large three-masted sailing ship. They told me we would sail south on the Atlantic Ocean to the very tip of South America, round Cape Horn, and then sail northward to California. Father had said the journey would take four long months.

"Clara, is your trunk packed?" Father's voice startled me.

I pushed the boot trunk out of my room. For a few minutes, I stood in the doorway of my room taking one last look. I shut the door. I pushed my trunk to the end of the hall and left it there for father to carry down the stairs.

Slowly, I walked down the stairs. When I reached the bottom, there stood dear Mrs.

Murphy, our landlady. I loved Mrs. Murphy. She was my friend and she always smelled like fresh-baked cinnamon buns. Her eyes flooded with tears. She dabbed at her eyes with the corner of her apron and sniffled. "Clara, I have made something for you."

Mrs. Murphy handed me a large white linen hankie with the initial C embroidered on one corner. Blue flowers coiled in and out of the C.

"Clara, I embroidered this hankie especially for you. The blue periwinkles mean friendship because we will always be friends, no matter how far away you go!" Tears poured down her face.

As I tucked the hankie into my pocket, I almost giggled. Maybe Mrs. Murphy needed the hankie more than I did. Then a terrible thought jumped into my mind. Maybe I *would* need the hankie when I reached the dock. As I thanked Mrs. Murphy, she slipped the handle of a big basket over my arm. She told me to look inside. When I lifted the lid of the basket, I *knew* I would need Mrs. Murphy's hankie.

Chapter Two

Aboard Ship

In the basket I saw a small black and white kitten sound asleep. Mrs. Murphy hugged me close and said, "This kitten will be your friend, Clara, on your long sea journey to California."

I looked at the small fuzzy ball in the basket. He opened his eyes. He looked just like Callie. Now, maybe I wouldn't miss Callie so much!

Mrs. Murphy walked me to the front porch and watched as Father helped Mother and me climb into the waiting carriage. A small group of our friends and neighbors had gathered to say goodbye to us.

Jack, the freckle-faced boy next door, stood near the horses making faces at me. He always made funny faces when he wanted to get my attention. I wouldn't miss him, but I'd miss Dixie, his big yellow dog. Everytime I patted Dixie's big head, Jack would chase me and try to yank my curls. One day when Jack was chasing me, I got so mad that I stopped running, turned around, and ripped the woolen sweater he was wearing right

Right away I knew Captain Nickels was a kind man and not like some of the mean sea captains I'd read about in my adventure books.

off his back! I had never seen Jack so mad. He started yelling at the top of his lungs, "My grandmother made this sweater for me. Clara Frances Allen, you're going to get it when I tell my grandmother about this!"

"Poor old Jack!" I thought. "Who would he chase now?"

I couldn't look at my best friend, Eileen. I was afraid I would start crying all over again. Eileen and I had always been friends. We shared books, games, and secrets. I would miss her. I'd miss all the fun times we'd had together . . . running along the seashore, gathering shells, hiding from Jack, and teasing Eileen's little brother.

After many tears and good-byes, the driver turned the horses around and we started toward the docks. The horses' hooves clip-clopped, clip-clopped on the cobblestone streets. We waved to our friends until we could see them no more. We passed the farmers' market where the first shopkeepers were putting out their goods. It was early morning and I could smell the shellfish already boiling in large black kettles. From the brick ovens, the smell of fresh baked bread filled the air. Meats, fish, fruits, and vegetables were being unloaded in the marketplace. I saw my father smile as a merchant unloaded sacks of coffee beans. "I'll miss the taste of a good cup of

Boston coffee!" he said.

Mother and I waved to Tilly as we passed her colorful flower stand. Tilly ran alongside our carriage and tossed small bunches of purple violets into our laps. "Good-bye Clara! Good-bye Elsie!" she cried. "Good-bye Pearlie! I'll miss you all."

Soon the cobblestone streets ended and we came to the harbor. The sun had broken through the fog and we could see a large three-masted sailing ship anchored in the bay.

Father spoke excitedly, "Look, Clara! It is the square-rigger that will take us to California! Look at the size of that ship! It must be two hundred feet long! I am told that the captain has worked for many, many years for the Martin and Martin Shipping and Trading Company. He has such a good reputation that the ship's owners allowed him to help design the ship."

Our trunks were loaded into a small ship's boat. A sailor helped us into the boat and rowed us out to the large sailing ship.

As we came closer to the square-rigger, I tilted my head back and looked up at the bow of the ship. There under the bowsprit, I saw a carved wooden figure of a lady holding a shell to her lips. Her brightly painted golden hair and her long blue gown made her look almost real. Below the lady was printed the ship's name, *Lady Shellhorn*.

I heard a shout! A man standing on the deck of the square-rigger motioned for us to come aboard. He was tall and a dark beard covered most of his face. He wore a navy blue suit with gold buttons. As I carefully climbed to the top of the accomodation ladder, his large hand reached for mine. Holding my hand tightly, he gently helped me step on board ship. In a flash he removed his navy blue cap from his head and politely bowed to me.

"Hello, little lady, I'm Captain Nickels. What is your name?"

I stood as straight and tall as I could. "My name is Clara Frances Allen," I said, "and I'm nine and a half years old!"

"Pleased to meet you, Miss Clara Frances Allen," he said as he shook my hand.

Right away I knew he was a kind man and not like some of the mean sea captains I'd read about in my adventure books. I stood next to the captain and watched as the sailors loaded the last of the cargo through the main hatch into the hold of the ship. I reached into my skirt pocket and pulled out my journal. I couldn't wait to start writing about Captain Nickels and the excitement I felt about being on board the *Lady Shellhorn*.

Captain Nickels greeted my parents as they

came aboard. He told them that we were the only passengers on board his three-master. Mother and Father enjoyed meeting the captain. I could tell that Mother was excited about being aboard the *Lady Shellhorn*. She couldn't wait to ask a question.

"What is the large beam that sticks out from the bow of the ship and why is the end of the beam decorated with the face of a cat?"

"That beam is called the cat head," said Captain Nickels as he pointed in the direction of the bow. "There is one on either side of the bow. The sailors believe that the cat faces painted at the end of the beams bring us good luck. The cat heads are important when we raise the anchors out of the water. The cat heads hold the anchors away from the side of the ship and keep the anchors from smashing against the ship."

"Thank you, Captain Nickels. I know we can learn a lot about sailing ships from you."

Next, he introduced us to his wife, Mrs. Nickels, who stood close by. Mrs. Captain, as I called her, smiled at us. She was a very pretty woman. She had curly blond hair and freckles across her face just like me. Mrs. Captain said, "Welcome. I'm glad to have you aboard the *Lady Shellhorn*. We rarely carry passengers and seldom a person as young as you, Clara."

I wondered if Mrs. Captain had any children. Did she have to leave them at home?

Mrs. Captain told us that she had always traveled with Captain Nickels on these trading journeys to California.

"Come with me," said Mrs. Captain, "and I'll show you where you will be making your home for the next four months."

As we walked along the creaking deck of the ship, Mrs. Captain noticed the red journal I held under my arm.

She laughed and said, "I see you've brought your journal, Clara. You will certainly have plenty to write about on this journey. Just wait until Mr. Simon, the sailmaker, and Sam-Lee, the cook, start telling you yarns. Their adventures will make your curly hair go straight!"

Mrs. Captain looked at my basket and raised one eyebrow in a question. I opened the lid of the basket and said, "This is my brand-new kitten. My friend, Mrs. Murphy, gave him to me this morning. She said that he would be my friend on the long journey. I've decided to name my kitten Murphy. I hope it is all right that he stays with me." I twisted one of my curls and pushed it back behind my ear while waiting for her answer.

"Of course, Clara," Mrs. Captain answered. "There are five cats on board this ship. Each one of them works hard to keep the rats and mice from destroying our cargo."

"Rats on board this ship?" I thought. The idea of meeting a rat in the dark did not make me happy. "Would there be rats in the cabin where I slept?"

Chapter Three

Our Home At Sea

On board the ship, Mrs. Captain took us to our cabin near the stern of the ship. She said that the cabin had been a storage room. In the cabin were a hammock, a small dresser with three drawers, a washstand, and a chamber pot. A set of bunk beds was under the port hole and another set of bunk beds was across the room. A coal-burning stove stood in one corner and a hurricane lamp was fastened to the wall. All the furniture and the stove were bolted to the floor so nothing could move during the sea journey. It was hard for me to believe that this tiny cabin would be our home for the next four months.

While Mrs. Captain talked to my parents, I peeked under the bunks and behind the stove to make sure there were no rats watching us with their little, black, beady eyes!

As Mrs. Captain opened the door to leave our cabin, I caught a glimpse of a boy dashing down the hall. "Who was that?" I asked.

"That was Asa, the cabin boy," said Mrs.

*As we followed Mrs. Captain to our cabin, I could see some of
the sailors unfurling the sails high in the yards.*

Captain. "He's a hard worker and a great help to the captain. About two years ago, he stowed himself away in a barrel aboard the *Lady Shellhorn*. By the time we discovered him, we were several days at sea. When he told us he had no family and had always wanted to go to sea, Captain Nickels and I decided to make him our cabin boy. He's quick to learn and because we do not have children of our own, Asa has become like a son to us. You'll meet Asa later, Clara." I wondered about Asa and why it was he wanted to go to sea.

The sailors pushed the poles on the large capstan that brought up the heavy anchor.

Chapter Four

"Haul Away, Joe"

August 10, 1845
Leaving Boston Harbor

As we finished unpacking our trunks, the shouts of the sailors told us that the *Lady Shellhorn* was about to sail. Mother, Father, and I rushed out on deck.

When we reached the deck, Father showed me how the wooden hatches had been closed and covered with canvas.

"The hatches need to be tightly covered, Clara, to keep the salt water from leaking into the hold below and damaging the supplies and cargo. When we are far out at sea, there will be storms and the winds will blow the waves over the decks and water will be everywhere."

"Maybe we should cover our doorway with canvas, too", I said.

Father looked at me and grinned. "No need for that, Clara. We will be safe and dry in our little cabin."

Captain Nickels called his crew and officers together. The captain and the first mate were the only two men who wore dark blue uniforms. The

*Haul Away, Joe

Short Haul Shanty

In this humorous shanty, the forceful pull on the ropes takes place on the word "Joe."

1. When I was a lit - tle lad and so my mo - ther told me,

'Way, haul a way, we'll haul a - way Joe! That

if I did - n't kiss the girls my lips would grow all mol - dy,

'Way, haul a way, we'll haul a - way Joe!

2. King Louis was the King of France before the Revolution,
   But then he got his head cut off which spoiled his constitution.

3. Once I was in Ireland a-diggin' turf and praties,*
   But now I'm on a Yankee ship a-haulin' sheets and braces.

4. Way, haul away, we'll haul for better weather,
   Way, haul away, we'll hang and haul together.

   * Praties = Potatoes

*The sea shanty "Haul Away, Joe" reprinted here with kind permission
from: Arlen, Karen, et al., *They Came Singing, Songs from California's
History*. Oakland, CA: Calicanto Associates, 1995, page 74.

sailors were dressed in turtleneck sweaters, well-worn trousers, and caps. Some wore black boots and others were in their bare feet. Each sailor carried a sheath knife on his belt.

We heard the captain tell the men how he expected each one to work hard, get along with one another, and obey the rules of the ship. Next, the first and second mates chose the men who would be on day watches and night watches. Before Captain Nickels dismissed the sailors, he spoke to them again. This time his voice was very serious. It was like my father's voice when he wanted me to pay close attention.

"Some of you men have never sailed with me. It is important that you know I expect all hands to do their duty to the best of their ability. We will be together more than 120 days and we must work as a team to make this a safe and successful journey."

Suddenly everything started happening at once! "Man the capstan!" ordered the captain.

"Aye, aye, sir! Man the capstan!" called the first mate.

The men were cheerful and eager to get out to sea. One of the sailors started to sing a shanty. I listened to the sailors sing "Haul Away, Joe!" as they worked. Singing together seemed to help them work faster.

"Heave away, my boys," called the first mate. The sailors sang as they pushed the poles on the large capstan that brought up the anchor.

I watched as the strong ropes circled about the capstan. I could see the anchor rise out of the water. The first mate cupped his hands around his mouth and shouted to the captain, "Anchor short, sir!"

"Very well," answered Captain Nickels. "Send some men aloft to unfurl the top sails."

"Aye, aye, sir!" answered the first mate. Sailors scrambled up the masts while the sailors on deck braced the yards by hauling on the lines fastened to the yardarms.

"Heave! O, heave! Heave and let go!" the sailors on deck chanted.

"One of you go aft and take the wheel," bellowed the second mate.

While the sailors were busy on deck, a small paddle-wheel towboat nosed our ship out of the harbor.

"Set the jibs!" ordered the captain.

When the jibs were set, the towboat took our hawser and began to tow our ship out into the open sea.

I listened to the ship's masts creaking and groaning as gusts of wind filled the sails. The sailors sang another shanty as they pulled on the lines and unfurled more sails. When I listened to the sailors' songs, I wanted to help pull on the lines, too.

Running under the bow of the *Lady Shellhorn*, the towboat cast off our hawser as the ship moved farther and farther out to sea. We waved good-bye to the pilot on the towboat.

We watched as Boston disappeared into the distance. The winds grew stronger and the *Lady Shellhorn* moved faster and faster. At last our fifteen-thousand-mile journey had started! We were on our way to California!

One of the sailors started to sing a shanty. I listened to the sailors sing "Haul Away, Joe" as they worked. Singing together seemed to help them work faster.

There were always men working the bilge pump. The pump was used to bring up water that seeped down through the decks into the lowest part of the ship's hull.

Chapter Five

Tour Of The Ship

August 11, 1845
At sea

We all slept well our first night at sea. I had the top bunk so I could see out of the porthole. The first thing I saw the next morning when I looked out was foamy green water rushing past the sides of our ship.

There was a knock on our cabin door. The sound of Mrs. Captain's voice filled the tiny cabin.

"Are you ready to tour the *Lady Shellhorn* with me?" she asked.

Within a few minutes, Mother, Father, and I were dressed and on deck where Mrs. Captain was waiting for us. "There you are," she said. "Did you sleep well? Were you warm enough? Did you hear the bilge pump this morning? Do you smell Sam-Lee's coffee? I'll bet you are hungry. Let's start our tour with the galley and get all of you some breakfast!" She spoke so quickly I could hardly understand what she was saying. I stood looking at her. I twisted a lock of my hair around my finger and wondered why she talked so fast.

Mrs. Captain scurried ahead motioning for us to follow. Suddenly she came to a stop. We almost fell over her. "This is the deck house," she said. "Mr. Simon, the sailmaker, has his workshop here and Mr. Turk, the ship's carpenter, is in the workshop next to him. On the other side of Mr. Simon, is the galley," she said.

From where I stood, I could see into the galley. The cook was busy. I could see his long, shiny black braid twisted around the top of his head.

One by one, we stepped into the small galley. Now I could see what the cook was doing. He was sprinkling flour on thick slabs of dough. Using a tin cutter, he cut out perfectly round biscuits faster than I could count them. I could already taste those golden brown biscuits hot from the oven!

"Meet Sam-Lee," said Mrs. Captain. As Sam-Lee turned to greet us, Mrs. Captain continued, "These are our passengers, Sam-Lee. This is Mr. and Mrs. Allen and their daughter, Clara. They will be taking all their meals here with you."

Sam-Lee smiled at each one of us and shook our hands. He immediately asked us to sit down at a small table. Mother, Father, and Mrs. Captain sipped hot coffee from tin mugs and I was given milk. We also enjoyed bowls of hot rice sprinkled with raisins. Mrs. Captain chatted on and I discovered that she and Captain Nickels had eaten breakfast in their cabin before dawn.

As we left the galley, I asked Sam-Lee, "When will we eat those biscuits?"

"Not until lunch," said Sam-Lee.

"Be on time because they disappear quickly," warned Mrs. Captain.

When we stepped back out on the deck, Mrs. Captain pointed to the bow of the ship.

"The crew lives in the forecastle under the bow. The sailors call it the fo'c'sl. There are bunks and hammocks for twenty sailors. There are always a few sailors asleep in the fo'c'sl because they sleep between their watches. They also do their washing, reading, and eating in their quarters."

She showed us a large barrel painted bright red. "Here is fresh drinking water for the sailors and you," she said. "Fresh water cannot be used for washing clothes, so you must do as the sailors do and use a bucket of salt water!"

"How do you get a bucket of salt water?" I said.

"Clara, always let a sailor get it for you. It is very dangerous to get salt water in a bucket. The sailors use a rope attached to the handle of a bucket and lower it down the side of the ship. Sailors have to be careful because they could fall overboard if they lose their balance. When you

The crew lives in the forecastle under the bow. The sailors call it the fo'c'sl. As we walked by the fo'c'sl, I noticed that it was a dark, three-cornered room in the ship's bow. A few sailors were asleep in the fo'c'sl because they sleep between their watches. Others were playing cards and talking.

wash your clothes, you will have to use a special soap that lathers up in salt water. You can buy saltwater soap from the slop chest where the sailors buy their soap and other supplies." I looked at mother. She looked at my father and they shook their heads. Saltwater soap and slop chests?

"Don't worry," said Mrs. Captain. "You'll soon get used to life on board ship!"

As we moved to the stern of the ship, I heard Mrs. Captain say that she and the captain ate all their meals in their own private quarters. Mrs. Captain invited us into their living quarters. We stepped into a large room with fancy chairs, a red velvet sofa, and a long wooden table covered with maps and charts. The bulkheads were covered with beautiful polished wood and a skylight above made the room bright and cheery.

I looked around the cabin and my mouth dropped open. In one corner of the room was an aviary that was built from the floor to the ceiling! It was filled with tiny birds of every color. Every bird watched Mrs. Captain.

"Come, everyone, and meet my birds. I collect birds from all over the world!"

My father gave a little whistle and some of the birds started to sing. "They like you, Pearlie," said Mrs. Captain.

Next to this room was the bedroom and a small bathroom. In the bathroom was a wash stand and a chamber pot. I was surprised to see a bathtub sitting on four clawed feet. I wondered how the tall captain could sit in that small tub? Wouldn't his long legs stick up out of the water? I turned to Mrs. Captain and giggled, but all I could say was, "Does the captain like saltwater baths?"

"Yes, he does, Clara. He says the hot salt water helps clear his stuffy head."

The sound of clinking silverware and china reached our ears. We followed Mrs. Captain back to the living room. There was the cabin boy that Mrs. Captain had told us about. What was his name again?

"Asa, I want you to meet Mr. and Mrs. Allen and their daughter, Clara." Asa looked at us and grinned from ear to ear.

I knew the minute Asa smiled that we would be friends.

"Lunch time, Clara," said my father. "Let's go to the galley and get some of Sam-Lee's biscuits! We don't want to wait too long or they'll all be gone!"

Chapter Six

My Friend, Asa

September 3, 1845
At sea

During the next several weeks we continued to sail southward along the coast of North America and through the Caribbean Sea. The ship sailed day and night. I thought the ship would stop at many ports, but it didn't. After we left Boston the anchor was not dropped until we reached the port of Rio de Janeiro.

Asa and I had become good friends. Although he was busy most of the day, he always managed to have time to talk to me. He tried to teach me the names of the sails and the lines. The sails' names were easy to learn, but it was much harder to remember the names of the more than one hundred lines.

The first time Mother and I decided to do some washing, we asked Asa to take us to the slop chest to buy some saltwater soap. The slop chest was in a small room next to the passageway. The slop chest was like a large locker. It was filled with smoking pipes, tobacco, shoes, socks, shirts, hats, boots, jackets, trousers, thread, fishhooks,

Asa stood at the wheel of the ship. Behind the wheel was the gear box. The gears moved a long shaft that went below decks and was attached to the rudder.

saltwater soap, books, and writing paper.

"Here is the slop chest, ladies. Take what you need and leave your IOU."

Back on deck, Asa took off his shoes and stood barefoot on the railing! Using a long rope attached to the handle, he dropped a bucket into the ocean. Balancing himself carefully, he pulled up the pail of salt water and presented it to us without spilling a drop!

I wrote often in my journal about Asa. He was fourteen years old, almost five years older than I. Asa was tall and thin. He had coal black hair and brown eyes. Even though he was young, he knew everything about our ship.

Asa was nothing like my neighbor, Jack, back in Boston. Asa did not yank my hair, make faces at me, or call me names. Instead, he was like the brother I had never had.

Asa had never known his parents and he had run away to sea at the age of twelve. I remember that Mrs. Captain had told us how Asa had stowed away in a barrel. Asa told me that, when Captain Nickels and Mrs. Captain had found him hidden on the ship, they had decided not to put him off at the nearest port. Instead, they had kept him on board as their cabin boy.

One day I saw Asa at the wheel of the ship. He motioned for me to come aft. Standing next to

Even though Asa was young, he knew everything about our ship.
Asa liked to climb the standing rigging. He spent many hours high
above the deck furling and unfurling the large square sails.

Asa, I asked, "Are you really steering this ship?"

Asa laughed, "It's not hard, Clara, especially when the seas are calm."

"How do you know where the ship is going?"

Asa pointed to a large box a few feet in front of him.

"That is the binnacle box, Clara. Look in it. What do you see?"

I peeked into the box. "I see a large compass and an oil lamp," I answered.

"You're right, Clara. I have to watch the compass carefully to make sure the *Lady Shellhorn* is on course and heading in the right direction. If the ship should go the slightest bit off course, the helmsman would have to work extra hard to make up for his mistake. The oil lamp is lit at night so the helmsman can see the compass. In a heavy storm, the first mate may call for two men to steer the ship. It is very hard to keep the ship on course when it is being tossed about by wind and high waves. Sometimes the men lash themselves to an eye-bolt in the deck to keep from being swept overboard."

When the first mate returned and took the wheel, Asa and I walked across the deck. Suddenly, on the starboard side of the ship a school of flying fish appeared. As we stood watching, the fish jumped higher and higher in the air. They looked as if they were playing leapfrog with one another. Many of the fish took extra high flying leaps and several of them landed smack in the middle of the deck. Before we could make a move, Sam-Lee, his long black braid flapping behind him, raced past us waving the largest meat cleaver I had ever seen. As the fish flip-flopped on the deck, Sam-Lee leaped from fish to fish shouting as loud as he could. With each shout he spun his cleaver in the air and then whacked it down on a fish. Asa and I hollered and laughed at the sight of those fish being chased around the deck by the cook. Even the sailors were laughing, but no one dared get close to Sam-Lee!

At dinner that night we were not surprised to see the steaming bowls of fish chowder Sam-Lee served us. Father said it was the best flying fish chowder he had ever tasted. And it was!

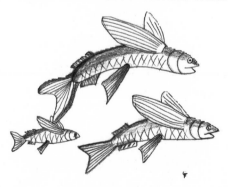

The flying fish looked as if they were playing leapfrog with one another.

Chapter Seven

Sam-Lee

September 10, 1845
At sea

Mother was seasick most of the time. She spent day after day resting in her bunk. The rolling motion of the ship made her very ill, but it did not seem to bother Father or me. Captain Nickels said that we had grown fine "sea legs," but Mother had not. Mother ate very little and did not join us for meals in the galley.

Each day, Father and I went to the galley to eat our meals. The captain and Mrs. Captain ate all their meals in their own cabin and the sailors ate in the fo'c'sl. Asa served meals to the captain and Mrs. Captain. The crew got their own food from Sam-Lee in the galley.

All the meals were cooked in the galley. It had a wood-burning stove with a Charlie Noble that went up through a hole in the overhead. In the galley near the stove was a small round table where we ate our meals. On the other side of the galley was a wooden work counter. Pots and pans, large spoons, ladles, wooden paddles, and a rolling pin hung over the counter. Below the

Sam-Lee was the ship's cook. He was not only a good cook,
but also our good friend.

counter were cupboards filled with supplies.

Sam-Lee was the ship's cook. He was not only a good cook, but also our good friend. He always saved tidbits for us to take back to Mother. One treat that Mother seemed to enjoy was duff, a sweet pudding flavored with molasses. A small bowl of duff always seemed to help her feel better.

While Father and I ate in the galley, we learned a lot about Sam-Lee. He told us he had come to America from China six years ago. He had come on a trading ship to the bay of San Francisco with his cousin.

When they arrived, Sam-Lee and his cousin, Kan-Lee, went to work for Mr. William Richardson who was a merchant in Yerba Buena. Sam-Lee and Kan-Lee learned to speak English by listening carefully and repeating some of the words that Mr. Richardson spoke.

One day several years ago while Sam-Lee was waiting for supplies to be unloaded from a trading ship, he had overheard Captain Nickels talking to Mrs. Captain. They were looking for a new cook to hire on board their ship. Sam-Lee had introduced himself to Captain Nickels and told the captain that he would like the job as cook.

Since that day, Sam-Lee had been the chief cook

on board the *Lady Shellhorn*. Mrs. Captain taught Sam-Lee how to cook for the captain and for the sailors. Sam-Lee learned how to make stew, beans, soup, biscuits, and duff. Although Sam-Lee cooked food that the sailors liked, he always managed to add his own special touches using dried herbs that he had collected at different ports.

Sam-Lee knew exactly which herbs to use in cooking. He also had special herbs that he put into boiling water to make tea. Sam-Lee told me that each tea had a special use. Some cured headaches, others helped backaches and swollen joints. There was always a pot of tea brewing on the back of Sam-Lee's stove. Sometimes the tea smelled sweet and spicy and other times the tea made me think of a musty old closet.

"How did you learn so much about herbs?" I asked Sam-Lee.

"My grandfather lived in Peking, China. He was one of the cooks at the emperor's palace."

Do you mean your grandfather cooked for the Emperor of China?"

"Yes, Clara. The emperor had many cooks, but my grandfather was his favorite. My grandfather learned what foods pleased the emperor and he prepared them with special herbs. When I was a young boy, I helped my grandfather gather herbs to use in the emperor's food. As we walked in the fields near Peking looking for herbs, my grandfather told me how he used each herb. I learned much about herbs from my grandfather."

After Sam-Lee told me about his grandfather, I paid special attention to every type of herb that Sam-Lee used. I asked him the names of the herbs and how to use each one. Someday I want to be a good cook like Sam-Lee.

Breakfast was my favorite meal of the day. Sam-Lee always had hot biscuits ready for us. Father and I split our biscuits open and spread each half with a thick layer of berry jam. When the chickens on board the ship laid extra eggs, Sam-Lee served fried eggs and bacon. At other times he put large scoops of bubbling oatmeal into our bowls. Often there was a tin of hardtack on our table. The taste of these hard dry sea biscuits was new to me, but I learned to like them.

When Father and I went to the galley at noon, I always knew what would be served . . . bowls of hot soup. One day we would have chicken soup full of rice and beans and on other days the soup would be thick with potatoes and onions. Guess what was always floating in the soup? Sam-Lee's special touches . . . herbs!

Dinner was often stew made from dried beef or perhaps fish and served with boiled potatoes or rice. Father always had hot coffee with his meals. I drank a special sweet tea that Sam-Lee brewed just for me.

I liked visiting with Sam-Lee in the galley. Not only was it warm and filled with good smells, but Sam-Lee always had funny stories to tell. I also liked his magic tricks. He pulled shiny gold coins from behind my ears and he could make a spoon stick to his nose. He was good at juggling, too. Why, he could juggle five small boxes at one time without dropping any of them.

One day when he finished juggling the boxes, Sam-Lee lined them all up in front of me.

"Clara, pick out your favorite box."

I had a hard time choosing one . . . they were all so handsome. Each one was painted with a different picture. One box had the Great Wall of China painted on it. Another had the Emperor of China's palace. There was a panda bear on a third box and a turtle on a fourth. The box I chose had a beautiful black and gold fish on it. I shook the box and could hear something inside.

"What is making the noise inside this box, Sam-Lee?"

"If you can figure out how to open the box, Clara, you may have it and the gift that is inside it." I turned the box over and over and pressed every corner, but I could not figure out how to open it.

Sam-Lee left the box on a shelf in the galley. Every day I tried to open it and every night I wrote in my journal that I had not yet learned the secret of Sam-Lee's mysterious little box.

José and Carmen Garcia de los Olivos were Spanish dancers on their way to Yerba Buena.

Chapter Eight

Rio de Janeiro

We sailed into the port of Rio de Janeiro on a clear springlike day. A towering rock stood guard over the harbor. Crescent-shaped sandy beaches stretched as far as I could see. Our ship anchored in the beautiful blue bay, and soon I saw the ship's boat being lowered into the water. Several sailors rowed Captain Nickels to shore. I watched from the deck until the ship's boat was out of sight. I wondered when they would come back.

The captain and the sailors were gone all day. Father told me that the captain would be busy making arrangements for fresh water and food.

That evening, Mother and Father and I were standing on the deck looking at the star-studded skies. The skies looked like black velvet and the stars shone like diamonds. Father was pointing out the constellations in the sky when we heard the splashing of the returning ship's boat. Captain Nickels and two strangers climbed the rope ladder to the deck of the ship. The sailors unloaded barrels of fresh water and several large stalks of green bananas. Baskets filled with red and yellow fruit were brought aboard. Colorful birds with long, beautiful tail feathers squawked noisily as their cages were hoisted aboard ship.

Before long, Captain Nickels introduced us to the man and woman he had brought on board ship. They were José and Carmen Garcia de los Olivos. The captain told us that they were Spanish dancers on their way to Yerba Buena and would be sharing our cabin.

I stared at the two new passengers. José wore a white shirt and a short black jacket with silver buttons. His black trousers were tucked into black leather boots that had fancy carved designs on the sides. Carmen wore a black hooded cloak. From under the cloak peeked a lacy red skirt that rustled when she moved. On her feet she wore bright red high-heeled shoes. It must have been very hard for Carmen to climb the ladder to the deck of the *Lady Shellhorn*.

"Buenas noches, mis amigos," said José and Carmen as they shook our hands.

Carmen smiled at me and reached down to pet Murphy.

"Qué gatito tan curioso!" she laughed. "Dónde está la mamá del gatito?"

"My wife wants to know where the funny little cat's mother is?"

"Murphy's mother lives in Boston and now I am his mother," I said quickly. Everyone started laughing and talking, but I wondered how two more people and their two big trunks would fit into our little cabin!

Mr. Simon's hands never stopped working. His hands moved back and forth, pushing the needle in and out of the heavy canvas.

Chapter Nine

Mr. Simon, The Sailmaker

October 3, 1845
At sea

One morning at eight bells, as the watch changed, I came on deck with Murphy to see what was happening. As I walked across the deck past the chicken coops, I saw Mr. Simon, the sailmaker, sitting outside the deck house by his workshop door. Walking toward Mr. Simon, I saw sailors hard at work. Some were polishing the brass rails, some were coiling the lines, and some were tightening the rigging. Mr. Simon was sitting on a sea chest with a large piece of canvas, a needle, and a chunk of beeswax. He was hard at work as usual.

I sat down next to him. "Why is the deck so white this morning?" I asked. Mr. Simon looked at me over the top of his tiny, wire-rimmed glasses.

"Clara, every morning while you are still asleep in your cabin, the sailors on the last watch of the night are told by the mate to 'turn to and wash down the decks!' You've never seen such activity, Clara. The pump is started and the barefooted crew roll their patched trousers above their knees. With brooms and brushes, they scrub the decks with sand and seawater. This morning the sailors used a holystone to give the decks an extra scrub. That is what made the decks so white."

As I listened to Mr. Simon explain about washing the decks, his hands never stopped working. They moved back and forth, pushing the needle in and out of the heavy canvas. Once in a while, he would stop to push the sewing cord through the beeswax to make the cord slick. The heavy cord Mr. Simon used was nothing like the smooth thread my mother used on her Boston quilting.

After he finished the story about the decks, I asked Mr. Simon what he was doing.

He said, "I'm making a Donkey's Breakfast."

"Do we have donkeys aboard this ship?" I asked.

"No, Clara," he said, putting down his canvas and taking a long sip of hot coffee from his tin cup. "Let me tell you about a Donkey's Breakfast. Remember the short storm we had a few days ago? The rain and the waves on the ocean brought a lot of water over the deck and much of the water drained down into the crew's quarters in the fo'c'sl. A lot of the crew's clothing got very wet. The worst part was that their mattresses were soaked with seawater and several of the mattresses were rotted and torn. Some of the sailors couldn't sleep on their beds and asked me to make new mattresses for them. That's what I'm doing, Clara. I sew these six foot long pieces of canvas into the shape of a sack. I leave an opening at one end of the sack so the sailors can stuff it with dry straw. Each sailor calls his mattress a Donkey's Breakfast."

As I sat laughing at Mr. Simon's story, I noticed Murphy chasing a large brown bug across the deck.

"What is Murphy chasing, Mr. Simon?" I asked.

"Why, that's a pesky cockroach that's traveling with us to California," chuckled Mr. Simon. "There are lots of cockroaches in the fo'c'sl. They love to make their beds in the straw mattresses. At night you can hear the cockroaches' feet scratching as they move around the cabin. If you light the lantern fast enough, you can see herds of them moving shoes and socks across the room. Remember, Clara, every morning you should shake your shoes and socks well before you put them on. You don't want any cockroaches to bite your toes!"

As my mouth dropped open, Mr. Simon continued talking.

"I remember the first trip I took on board a ship.

We not only had cockroaches sharing our beds, but also weevils who shared our hardtack. The hardtack was wormy with weevils. We would pound the hardtack into pieces and drop the pieces into our tins of hot coffee. Soon the weevils would float to the top and we would spoon them off. After that we ate the softened hardtack and drank the coffee."

"Yukkk!" I said. I looked down into Mr. Simon's tin cup.

Could this be one of those *hair-raising* yarns that Mrs. Captain had warned me about? I looked at Mr. Simon carefully. Was he telling me the truth?

Chapter Ten

Child Overboard

October 11, 1845
A storm at sea

The *Lady Shellhorn* pushed her way through the stormy Atlantic Ocean. Her bow dipped in and out of the heavy swells. Holding tightly to the wheel, the first mate fought to keep the ship on course. In spite of the tremendous blasts of wind, the sailors climbed the masts to take in the main sail.

An enormous sea rose. The ship rolled and pitched from side to side. The ship would roll far to the port side, come upright, and then roll far to the starboard side. The wind grew stronger. Rain poured out of the dark clouds. Lightning lit up the skies.

The decks filled with water as huge waves crashed over the bow of the ship. A lifeline was stretched fore and aft so that the sailors would have something to hold onto as they worked to keep the ship afloat.

In our stuffy cabin we could hear orders being shouted to the crew. The sounds of ripping canvas and waves crashing on the deck filled our

An enormous sea rose. The decks filled with water as huge
waves crashed over the bow of the ship. A lifeline was stretched
fore and aft so that the sailors would have something to hold onto
as they worked to keep the ship afloat.

ears. Mother, Father, and I lay in our bunks holding on to the side boards. Mother's face was very pale. She moaned with each roll of the ship. José and Carmen sat side by side in their bunk holding onto each other. With every lurch of the ship, Carmen grabbed her stomach and groaned. Outside the cabin door, we could hear heavy rain pounding on the deck. The wind howled like a wild animal and sent shivers down my spine. Wo-o-o-o-o! Wo-o-o-o-o! This was the wildest ride I'd ever had.

We had to stay in our cabin for almost two days. Late in the afternoon of the second day, the storm seemed to calm down and I noticed patches of blue sky through my porthole. Father decided that it was safe to go out on deck. He helped me put on my warm red coat and bundled up my mother in her wool sweater and scarf. Carmen and José joined us as we stepped out of the cabin onto the wet, slippery deck. Grasping the handrails, we carefully stepped over tangled ropes and clumps of brown seaweed. Above our heads several torn sails told us that Mr. Simon would soon be very busy.

I stood at the rail with the fresh sea air blowing against my face. The sea air made me feel much better and I noticed the color in Mother's face had returned.

Sam-Lee came on deck with a basket and handed each one of us pieces of fruit, hardtack, and beef jerky. My mouth begin to water when I saw the ripe fruit. I took a bite of banana, a bite of jerky, and a bite of hardtack. This was the first food I had eaten in two days and to me it was a feast!

"I'm going to take a scrap of beef jerky to Murphy," I yelled as I ran in the direction of the cabin.

"Be careful! The decks are slippery! Come right back, Clara. It's getting dark," warned Mother.

As the sun set, the sails of the ship lost their rosy glow and long shadows danced across the deck. In the gathering darkness, it was hard to see. Suddenly, a blast of wind caused the ship to roll to one side. Something red slid across the deck and disappeared overboard.

The first mate saw the flash of red go up and over the railing. What was that? Was that a person? Clara? Wasn't she wearing a red coat?

Without wasting a second, the first mate bellowed, "Child overboard! All hands on deck!"

Sailors still wearing oilskins and sou'westers appeared from the fo'c'sl. Running to their stations, they awaited orders from the first mate. Some of the men grabbed the railings and looked off into the darkness, their sharp eyes scanning the water.

The first mate's orders flew quickly from one sailor to the next. "Get the captain!" was hollered at Asa. Asa jumped to attention as if struck by lightning and ran to the stern of the ship. After a quick knock on the captain's door, and without waiting to be told to enter, Asa burst into the captain's cabin.

In a high-pitched, excited voice, Asa yelled, "Captain! Captain! Come quickly! Someone's overboard! They think it may be Clara!"

Captain Nickels and his wife sat at the far end of the long wooden table surrounded by maps and books. Yelling, "Child overboard!" Asa grabbed the back of the high-backed chair right in front of him and swung it around to step closer to the captain.

There I sat on the high-backed chair! Asa stared at me in disbelief and babbled words that no one could understand. "Wha . . . , wha . . . , wha?"

The captain jumped up, knocking over his chair. He took one huge step and stood directly in front of Asa. Bending down so his face was only inches from Asa's face, Captain Nickels growled, "Speak clearly! Spit it out! Say it now!" Shaking from head to toe, Asa swallowed hard and pointing to me he cried, "Wha...,wha...,wha...what's she doing here? Everybody thinks she's overboard!"

The captain grabbed his silver megaphone and yelled for all of us to follow him. We raced out the cabin door! Captain Nickels bellowed into the megaphone, "All hands, hold fast! Clara is found! Hold fast!"

As all eyes turned to look at me, I stepped out from behind the captain. Immediately my mother and father rushed toward me and Father scooped me up in his arms. Holding lanterns, sailors surrounded us. A voice from high above in the crow's nest could be heard shouting, "Hooray for Clara! Hooray for Clara!"

Chapter Eleven

Where Is Murphy?

October 13, 1845
At sea

I woke up early the next morning clutching the locket that hung around my neck. In all the excitement of last night I was lucky not to have lost it. I opened my hand and looked at the gold, heart-shaped locket. It had my name on it . . . *Clara*.

I sat up in my bunk. I could feel the gentle rocking of the ship. The creaking of the ship's boards reminded me of the terrible storm. The happenings of the day before drifted through my head. Had I been dreaming? No, it had not been a dream.

From underneath my pillow I pulled out my leather-bound red journal. As I did every morning, I turned to a fresh page, put the date at the top, and began writing.

Yesterday had been a wild day. It had all started in the late afternoon when we had gone on deck after the storm. I remember telling my mother that I was taking a scrap of jerky to Murphy who was asleep in our cabin.

*I sat up in my bunk. From underneath my pillow I pulled out
my red journal and began writing.*

When I reached our cabin, the door was wide open and Murphy was gone. I had to find him before it got darker. Had he gotten into some kind of trouble? What was I going to do? I thought of the one person who could help me find my kitten . . . Captain Nickels.

On the way to Captain Nickels's cabin, I felt the ship roll to one side. I lost my balance and fell over the red barrel that held the drinking water. The barrel had come unbolted from the deck during the storm. As I stood up, the red barrel rolled past me. In a flash, it rolled across the deck and flipped up and over the railing into the ocean.

When I knocked on the captain's door, his deep voice told me to enter. I opened the door slowly and peeked into his cabin. Captain Nickels and his wife were using a measuring instrument on a large map spread out on the table in front of them. Without looking up, the captain had pointed to a large high-backed chair. I climbed onto the chair and sat waiting for the captain to finish his work.

The next thing I remember was the captain's door flying open and the shouts of Asa, as he yanked my chair around. I barely remember someone grabbing my hand and pulling me through the doorway. All at once I was on deck surrounded by sailors who kept telling me how lucky I was that I hadn't fallen overboard. I hadn't even *thought* about falling overboard! I tried to tell everyone that I was just looking for my kitten, Murphy.

Suddenly, I stopped writing in my journal. A horrible thought came back to me. Had anyone found Murphy? I had been so tired last night that I had fallen asleep not even thinking about my poor cat. In all the excitement I hadn't had a chance to ask the captain about my missing cat. Where was Murphy? Had *he* fallen overboard?

Chapter Twelve

Carmen's Trunk

October 13, 1845
At sea

I closed my journal. I couldn't write any more. Thinking about Murphy made me sad. As I tucked my leather journal back under my pillow, I heard a scratching noise coming from across the small cabin. That wasn't a ship noise! I twisted a lock of my hair around my finger and thought hard.

Again I heard the noise. I just had to have a look! Slowly I climbed down from my bunk, being very careful not to disturb my mother and father who were still sound asleep in the bunk below me. I tiptoed over to the blanket that we hung up at night to divide the room. I lifted the blanket. There, directly in front of me was Carmen's bunk. As she slept, her left arm hung over the edge of the bunk. There must have been one hundred silver bracelets dangling on her arm. Where did Carmen get so many bracelets? I looked at her long, curly black hair that poured like black ink over her white pillow case. I had never seen such curly hair!

Thinking about Murphy made me sad.
What had happened to my poor little kitten?

José lay snoring in a hammock with his mouth wide open. As I tiptoed closer, I couldn't resist standing up and looking into José's open mouth. I couldn't believe what I saw. His mouth was filled with gold teeth! I counted ten of them!

I heard the funny noise again. I listened carefully. The noise was coming from Carmen's huge leather trunk. I wondered if a rat had gotten in there.

I dropped to my knees and crept close to the trunk. The heavy lid was slightly open. The painted heel of one of Carmen's bright red shoes was caught on the latch. I listened again. I could still hear scratching noises. I used both hands and slowly pushed up the heavy lid. A wonderful odor of roses came drifting out of the trunk. Then, what did I see? A tiny paw and a little pink nose poked its way over the edge of the trunk. There was Murphy half-buried in Carmen's lacy red petticoats. I reached in and pulled Murphy to my face. He smelled like roses. I had never been so happy to see anyone in my whole life!

*Just the sight of Blackbeard with his pistols and his long black beard
braided and tied with ribbons was enough to bring fear to the
hearts of the bravest sailors.*

Chapter Thirteen

Blackbeard The Parrot

October 20, 1845
The Atlantic Ocean

The captain had given one of the beautiful parrots that he had purchased in Rio de Janeiro to Mrs. Captain. The parrot had a piece of rope tied to his leg. The other end of the rope was attached to Mrs. Captain's wrist. She had taught Blackbeard to say "Ahoy!" "Walk the plank!" and "Pieces of eight!" Sometimes she would ask the parrot for a kiss and he would peck her on the cheek! The parrot's little black eyes would just shine when he crawled up on Mrs. Captain's shoulder and she asked him to talk. That bird had been so loud and squawky when he was first brought aboard ship that it was a wonder anyone would want him. Mrs. Captain in her usual kind way had petted and loved him with many kind words. It was no wonder that Blackbeard had learned to speak so well.

I loved walking on the deck of the *Lady Shellhorn* with Mrs. Captain and her talking parrot. At first I was afraid to touch Blackbeard, but gradually I learned to stroke his long silky feathers. He'd turn his head and look at me with one eye and when he squawked, the black feathers under his chin stood straight out. I asked Mrs. Captain, "Why did you name your parrot Blackbeard?"

"I call him by that name because the black feathers under his chin remind me of a famous pirate who lived many years ago named Blackbeard."

When I told Mrs. Captain that I had never heard of Blackbeard the Pirate, she looked surprised. She bent down and looked into my eyes. "Why Clara, let me tell you about the famous Englishman, Blackbeard the Pirate," she said.

*   *   *

Blackbeard the Pirate

Blackbeard was a pirate who lived in the early 1700s. He terrorized the towns and ships along the Atlantic coast from Boston to the Caribbean Sea.

Blackbeard began his pirating days in a very small longboat. He packed as many men as possible into the boat and sneaked up on a large trading ship. His men scrambled up the anchor chain of the trading ship in hopes of catching the ship's crew off guard. Though Blackbeard's men were outnumbered, they fought a fierce battle and won. Now the large trading ship they had attacked became the pirates' ship. Blackbeard re-named the ship Queen Ann's Revenge. The pirates celebrated their victory by gorging themselves on all the supplies stored on the ship. Within a week, all the food was eaten and now the pirates had to find other ships to raid.

Blackbeard's pirate ship hid in bays and rivers or behind tree-covered sand bars and fearlessly attacked all ships. As he sailed after the trading ships, he had a way of frightening sailors so badly they would shake in their boots. He would raise the pirate flag, the Jolly Roger. As the black flag with the white skull and crossbones flapped in the breeze, everyone who saw it knew that Blackbeard and his pirates were ready to attack. Just the sight of Blackbeard with his three sets of pistols strapped around his waist and his long black beard braided and tied with ribbons was enough to bring fear to the hearts of the bravest sailors.

All of the gold that Blackbeard took is said to be buried on islands throughout the Caribbean Sea. Once one of Blackbeard's men asked him where he had buried his money. He answered, "Nobody but Beelzebub and I know where the gold is hidden and the one who lives the longest should take all the gold."

* * *

The yarn had ended, but I thought about Blackbeard and his pirates sailing on the oceans. I wondered if Captain Nickels had ever seen a ship flying the Jolly Roger? What would Captain Nickels do if we were suddenly chased by a shipload of pirates? I looked at the parrot. He looked at me and slowly winked one eye!

Chapter Fourteen

Penguins Don't Fly

October 30, 1845
Punta Tombo, Argentina

Strong Atlantic winds were pushing our ship steadily southward. Mr. Simon, the sailmaker, was very busy making sure all the sails were in good working order. He told my father, Pearlie, that Captain Nickels had decided not to anchor at Punta Tombo in Argentina where he usually took on fresh water for the crew and passengers. Instead, the captain had decided not to waste any time. He wanted to use the good winds and head straight for Cape Horn, the very tip of the South American continent.

As the winds continued to push our ship down the coast, I noticed Captain Nickels standing on the starboard side of the ship. He was watching the coastline with his silver spyglass. What did he see I wondered? As if the captain had heard my thoughts, he motioned for me to come over to him.

"Clara, we are now passing a point of land called Punta Tombo. Since leaving the port of Rio de Janeiro, this is the closest we have sailed to

I watched the penguins through the spyglass.
I had never seen such funny birds.

land. We are able to come close to shore because the water here is so deep. Look carefully through my spyglass and you will see something you've never seen before."

I peered through the spyglass. At first all I could see was water. Then Captain Nickels helped me focus the spyglass and as I looked more carefully, I could see little black shapes zigging and zagging in the water near the shoreline.

"What are those things?" I asked.

With a smile on his face, Captain Nickels answered, "Those 'things,' as you call them, are a type of bird you've probably never seen before, Clara. Those birds are called penguins and they don't fly."

The captain took the spyglass and held it to his eye. He handed the spyglass back to me and told me to look at the penguins on the shore. He told me to hold the spyglass with both hands to keep it steady. With the captain's help, I began to see more clearly. Suddenly I could see thousands and thousands of penguins standing on shore. The captain was right. I had never seen such funny birds. Some of them marched down to the water like tiny soldiers dressed in black and white uniforms. I could see others waddling across the beach and diving into the ocean waves.

As I watched, Captain Nickels said, "I have seen

penguins many times on my sea journeys down the coast of South America. On my last trip around Cape Horn I stopped here in Argentina for water. At Punta Tombo I walked on the shore among the penguins. Those birds make more noise than you can imagine, Clara. They sound like donkeys . . . 'He-aw, He-aw.' The shore where all those penguins live smells like a barnyard! Every day they swim and play in the ocean and eat krill, their favorite food."

"Unfortunately, Clara," Captain Nickels said to me in a low voice, "many of those penguins you're looking at swim into the ocean for their dinner and never return to shore."

"Why not?" I asked.

"Because killer whales are also looking for *their* favorite dinner . . . penguins!"

Chapter Fifteen

Rounding Cape Horn

November 10, 1845
From the Atlantic to the Pacific

The next day was sunny and cold and very windy. The strong steady winds filled all the sails and moved the *Lady Shellhorn* faster than it had ever sailed before. The huge square-rigger seemed to glide like a feather over the choppy gray waters. I sat in my favorite place near Mr. Simon's sea chest where I could see everything that was happening on deck. I watched the crew as they obeyed the orders hollered at them by the first mate.

I heard the sails snap and crack above my head. The winds blew harder. The wind whipped across my face and I could taste the salty sea spray. I was frightened and excited at the same time. What an adventure I was having!

Suddenly, I felt a hand on my shoulder. It was Mrs. Captain! She cupped her hands over her mouth and bent close to my ear. Over the roar of the wind and waves, I could hear her say, "Clara, how lucky we are to have a clear day to see Cape Horn! Watch carefully because here it

*Finally it was happening. We were rounding Cape Horn. It was
a rocky island with a large, steep, rock mountain at one end.
I could see no trees and nothing green. It was a lonely looking
island sitting at the very tip of South America.*

comes!"

At first, all I could see were dozens of small rocky islands. No one lived on the islands. The few trees that I could see had been twisted into weird shapes by the never ending winds. Finally it was happening. We were rounding Cape Horn.

I stared at Cape Horn. It was a rocky island with a large, steep, rock mountain at one end. I could see no trees and nothing green. It was a lonely looking island sitting at the very tip of South America. Mrs. Captain spoke into my ear again.

"Clara, this is where the Atlantic Ocean and the Pacific Ocean meet."

We looked at the churning waters. The two angry oceans pushed and clawed at each other. The hissing and spitting noise of the waves made me think of a giant kettle of boiling water.

I turned to look for my parents. I could not believe what I saw. Many of the sailors had climbed the masts and were standing on the yardarms saluting Cape Horn. Everyone else was on deck waving and cheering. I jumped to my feet and cheered too! I knew this was a special moment for everyone on board the *Lady Shellhorn!*

From morning until night we continued to race the wind around the island of Cape Horn. Great rocks reared out of the water to look at us. These tall rocks stood by themselves in the churning seas like soldiers guarding a fort. They loomed over us. The huge dripping rocks looked like elephant heads, bear heads, and camel heads, their eyes staring at us through long, dark slits. As the *Lady Shellhorn* sailed by these mysterious rocks, it seemed that the dark animal eyes followed our every move. I shivered, not so much from the cold wind, but from the thought that we were being watched by these huge sea monsters.

I closed my eyes and opened them. I would not have missed this trip for anything. Never again would I see a sight like Cape Horn . . . the end of the world!

Chapter Sixteen

The Doldrums

November 24, 1845
The Pacific Ocean

Two weeks had passed since we had rounded Cape Horn. Everyone on board ship seemed much happier. We were halfway to California. Even Mother felt better. She started eating meals with us in the galley. Captain Nickels spent time on deck talking to us and watching the sailors as they tightened the rigging, worked the bilge pump, cleaned up the fo'c'sl, and worked aloft on the yards.

Many times Captain Nickels told us how lucky we had been to have had such beautiful clear weather going round the Horn. He said that most ships usually had to battle Antarctic gales and fog. In snowy or foggy weather some ships had taken as long as two months just to round the *tip* of Cape Horn! We had met strong currents where the Atlantic and Pacific Oceans came together, but for our ship, the trip round the Horn had been like flying on a cloud.

During the days on the peaceful Pacific Ocean, we traveled up the coasts of Chile and Peru,

Life aboard ship was different in the Doldrums. Many of the sailors were sitting on deck. Some sat washing their clothes while others smoked their pipes and played cards.

sailing from cold to warmer weather. Now I could take off my shoes and stockings and wiggle my toes in the warm sun. The freckles on my nose and cheeks got so dark they looked like fleas.

At the end of each day, Mother, Father, and I strolled on deck and watched the sunset. Mother said that the sunsets on the ocean were the prettiest she had ever seen. I agreed. As the sun slowly disappeared below the watery horizon, streaks of brilliant red, crimson, orange, and yellow painted the sky. Little by little we watched as the bright colors faded away leaving us between day and night.

Every evening when we watched the day turn to night, Father took Mother and me by the hand and gave thanks for our lives and our safety on the ocean. He also gave thanks for the captain and the crew who masterfully sailed the *Lady Shellhorn*.

One morning when I came on deck, I noticed the sailors were not working. The sails hung limp on the yards and the ship hardly moved. I looked over the rail and the water was gently splashing against the side of the ship. I wondered what was happening. Why weren't we moving?

I saw Asa and Mr. Simon playing checkers on the old sea chest so I walked across the deck to talk with them.

"Why aren't we moving?" I asked.

"Well, Clara, we have hit the Doldrums," answered Mr. Simon. "We are close to the country of Ecuador and very near the equator. Sometimes in this part of the ocean it is very calm. There are no winds. So here we sit in the Doldrums waiting for a breeze to fill the sails and move the *Lady Shellhorn*."

Twisting a lock of hair around my finger, I thought about Mr. Simon's words. "What is Captain Nickels doing about this?" I asked.

"Just like everyone else, Captain Nickels is waiting for the slightest puff of wind. Then he will order the sailors to unfurl every sail on the ship and we hope, we will be on our way again!" Mr. Simon yawned and turned back to his checker game. I could tell he was already tired of being in the Doldrums.

On the quarterdeck I saw Father talking to Captain Nickels. I decided to join them. When I reached my father's side, he smiled at me and put his hand on my shoulder. Captain Nickels was explaining the parts of the ship, the hull, the masts, the sails, and the rigging. He told us how each part of the ship helped the other parts. If any part were weak and did not work, the whole ship would be in danger. Captain Nickels told us about the ship's wooden hull and how washing the decks every day kept the wooden planking from drying out. If the decks dried out, the ship would start to leak!

Father asked about the three tall masts. Captain Nickels showed him how the standing rigging kept the masts steady in the wind. Each mast held four large sails. All the sails were made of heavy canvas with a rope edging to make them strong. Each sail had many lines connected to it called the running rigging. As the wind changed, the sailors used the running rigging to move the sails into different positions to catch the wind.

As I looked up at the big square sails hanging limp on the yards, I had a sudden thought. "Captain Nickels, why do the sails at the bow of the ship have a different shape from the sails above us?"

"First of all, Clara, those three sails at the bow of the ship are called jibs. Each jib is cut in the shape of a triangle. One edge of the jib is extra long and full. When the jibs fill with wind, they give extra power to the ship."

"That's interesting, Captain Nickels. I think I'll go forward to the bow and take a closer look at those jibs."

I walked toward the bow of the ship. Many of the sailors were sitting on deck. Some sat talking while they patched their worn clothes. Others smoked their pipes and played cards. I noticed two sailors with many pieces of ivory playing a game I had never seen before.

I missed the usual hustle and bustle. Life aboard ship certainly was different in the Doldrums.

Chapter Seventeen

Monkey Business

November 24, 1845
The Doldrums

Sam-Lee was standing near the bowsprit looking down into the water. He waved to me and called excitedly, "Come quickly, Clara!" When I reached his side, I looked over the railing. There in the water I saw two huge sea turtles.

"Those are the biggest turtles I've ever seen!" I said. "Each one is bigger than the captain's bath tub!"

"You are right about that, Clara," answered Sam-Lee. "I think they each weigh about three hundred pounds and they would make great soup! Have you ever eaten turtle soup, Clara? It tastes just like beef gravy."

"Ugh-ah-ah!!! Never!" I exclaimed.

For over an hour, we watched the turtles calmly swimming near the ship. Their big flippers hardly rippled the water and their greenish shells glistened in the sunlight. Both turtles seemed very happy to have the *Lady Shellhorn* keeping them company, if only for a little while. Now I was glad we were in the Doldrums. If the wind

For over an hour we watched the turtles swimming near the ship.
Their big flippers hardly rippled the water and their greenish
shells glistened in the sunlight.

had been up, we would have sailed swiftly past these large sea creatures and never have noticed them.

"Where do you think the turtles live? Do you suppose they have a home on land?" I asked Sam-Lee.

"The turtles live here in the ocean, Clara. They go ashore when they are ready to lay their eggs."

We continued to watch the turtles. At last, the turtles decided to leave us. As they swam away, I said, "Wouldn't it be fun to ride on the back of a turtle?"

"Ride on a turtle's back? Say, that reminds me of a yarn," said Sam-Lee.

"About a year ago, not far from here, Captain Nickels anchored the *Lady Shellhorn* off the coast of Costa Rica. I helped row the ship's boat to shore. The four sailors and the captain went into town. I decided to explore the tidepools along the beach."

"I was turning over rocks looking for tender bits of seaweed or perhaps a small octopus when I heard blood-curdling howls coming from the nearby jungle. 'Yi-i-i-i-i-! Whu-u-u-u-u! R-r-r-r-r!' Suddenly, before I knew what was happening, a monkey almost as large as you, Clara, bounded out of the jungle and with one huge leap, snatched my canvas bag right off my shoulder.

Then he headed back toward the jungle carrying my bag. That made me mad!"

"Weren't you scared, Sam-Lee?"

"I was too mad to be scared. I chased after that monkey and yelled so loudly that the monkey stopped, turned toward me, and dropped my bag on the ground! As I leaned over to grab my bag, the monkey took another leap and landed on my back! I ran around in circles trying to make him let go. I jumped up and down! I could feel his sharp teeth and long fingers digging into my neck and back. He howled louder and louder. 'Y-i-i-i-i! Whu-u-u-u-u! R-r-r-r-r!' I dashed to the ocean and plunged into the waves. Finally, the monkey let go."

"The last I saw of him he was standing on his hind legs at the edge of the jungle still howling and screeching at me."

"Did that really happen to you, Sam-Lee?"

Without another word, Sam-Lee pulled his shirt collar away from his neck. There on the side of his neck, I saw two long, dark scars.

"Clara, I'd rather take a ride on a turtle anytime than have a monkey take a ride on me!"

Chapter Eighteen

A Little Excitement!

November 27, 1845
The Doldrums

The days in the Doldrums were long and hot and humdrum. No one seemed to have any spunk. Even the chickens stopped laying eggs. The only time anyone showed any energy was when the sailors pumped seawater over the decks several times a day to keep them from drying out.

I spent long hours at the ship's railing staring out at the Pacific Ocean. Everything was quiet and still, just like a painted picture. As far as the eye could see there was water and more water every where. Before sailing into the Doldrums, we had sailed about one hundred and fifty miles a day. Now we were lucky to journey thirty or forty miles a day.

Mr. Turk, the ship's carpenter, sat on a pile of coiled rope whittling a piece of wood. I noticed he was using the sharp knife he always kept in a sheath attached to his belt.

"What are you whittling, Mr. Turk?"

"I'm whittling an albatross, Clara. Some people call it a gooney bird. He is the largest of all the

Asa sat in the bosun's chair that hung under the bowsprit.
He was painting the figurehead of the Lady Shellhorn.

seabirds." Mr. Turk held the half-carved figure up so I could see it.

"The bill of the albatross is long and powerful and his wingspread is often nine to eleven feet across."

"Is that an albatross that has been following our ship for the past few days?"

"No, it's not, Clara. We are too close to the equator to see an albatross. The bird that is following us is a brown pelican. He is waiting for Sam-Lee to throw scraps of food overboard."

"What is that big pouch under the pelican's bill?"

"Clara, you certainly ask a lot of questions. Why don't you go ask Asa about pelicans? He's with a very special lady! Look under the bowsprit and you'll find him!"

Asa was sitting in the bosun's chair that hung under the bowsprit. He was painting the figurehead of the *Lady Shellhorn*.

I leaned over the bowsprit. "Do you need some help, Asa? I like to paint."

"No thanks, Clara. You just stay put. It's much too dangerous down here for you. You might lose your balance and fall into the ocean."

As I watched Asa carefully painting the lady's golden hair, I noticed a black pointed fin in the water just below him. Three more black fins appeared. I knew what they were. Asa was too busy to notice.

"Sharks! Sharks! Asa! There are sharks below you!"

Asa looked down and then looked up at me. His face turned white. I moved fast! I grabbed the rope that held the bosun's chair. With all my strength, I pulled it toward me. As the chair moved up, it swung to the side of the ship. Asa threw his long legs up and over the railing. I grabbed his belt and pulled him to safety just as a huge shark lunged out of the water at him. The shark's wide-open mouth missed Asa's legs by a few inches, but its glistening white teeth clamped shut on the can of paint that hung from the bosun's chair.

Asa lay panting on the deck. I knelt down beside him and patted him on the back. "You'll never forget that shark, Asa, and he'll never forget you, either! That shark will always have a mouthful of golden teeth, thanks to you!"

Chapter Nineteen

Good-Bye To The Doldrums

November 27, 1845
Sailing again

That afternoon the skies darkened and a wall of rain moved toward us. Soon the deck was flooded with rainwater. The fresh water felt good on our upturned faces and tasted even better. Captain Nickels ordered the sailors to collect rainwater to put in the almost empty water barrels. John Turk used one of the running lines to haul up the corner of a sail so that it made a funnel. Rainwater ran down the funnel and poured into a large empty water barrel.

A gust of wind blew across the deck. Everyone looked up at the sails. Slowly each sail filled with fresh wind and we could hear the sound of rippling water along the bow. The *Lady Shellhorn* was headed north on the Pacific Ocean once again, leaving the Doldrums behind.

I couldn't believe how much cargo was in the hold of the ship. I saw hundreds of wooden barrels filled with tea, clocks, fans, dishes, spyglasses, and many other things.

Chapter Twenty

Below Decks

December 1, 1845
At sea

Can you imagine? It had happened again. Murphy was missing! He had been asleep beside me, at least, I thought he had been asleep, when I heard squawking by the chicken coop. Murphy had managed to squeeze into the coop and grab the wing of a large Rhode Island Red hen. She was furious!

"Squawk, squawk-aaa-kkk!" scolded the hen as she tried to keep Murphy away from her eggs. Peck! Peck! right on Murphy's nose. Murphy let out a loud "Meo-o-o-ww," squeezed out of the cage, and sprang up the closest line. In a second he was out of sight. That Murphy! Now who would help me find my cat? Mr. Simon? No, he was too busy repairing a large sail. Asa? He was too busy polishing all the brass railings on the ship. Sam-Lee? He was probably busy cooking some of his famous duff for Sunday dinner.

A shadow fell in front of me. It was Carmen. I knew she would help me look for Murphy. Carmen gave me a funny smile and pointed at the fringed shawl she was wearing around her shoulders. There was Murphy hanging by his sharp little claws on the back of the shawl. "Me-o-o-www," cried Murphy as he bounced onto the deck and dropped down the companionway. Carmen and I rushed after him, but he had vanished again. As we scrambled down the narrow companionway, we nearly fell over Mrs. Captain and Blackbeard. Blackbeard fluttered his wings to keep his foothold on Mrs. Captain's shoulder and squawked at us, "All hands on deck! Walk the plank! Walk the plank!"

Mrs. Captain asked, " Where are you girls going in such a rush?" When she heard what had happened, she laughed and said that she would help us search for Murphy.

Mrs. Captain led us to another narrow companionway that went down into the dark hold. Before we entered the hold, Mrs. Captain stopped to light a lantern that she carried with her. Carmen and I followed Mrs. Captain and the flickering lantern deep down into the ship. The smell of old, dirty socks filled the air. It made me feel sick. I pinched my nose.

"What is that awful smell?"

"It's bilge water," Mrs. Captain answered. "Seawater drips down from the upper decks and collects deep in the bottom of the ship. The sailors pump out as much as they can, but there is always some water left. It stagnates and smells. You'll get used to it, Clara."

"Aren't you afraid to come down here?"

"No, Clara, I come down here to check on the cargo and check for stray cats!" She smiled. Was she joking?

"Mrs. Captain," I said, "What is cargo?"

"Why Clara, the ship's cargo is all the things we are taking to Monterey and Yerba Buena for people to buy. There are saws and hammers, clothing and shoes, and furniture and lumber, and many more things. We even have a piano in the hold. A man in Yerba Buena wants to give it to his bride."

Mrs. Captain continued, "Clara and Carmen, would you both like to see some of our treasures? Perhaps you may see something you would like to have. Come along quickly and I'll show you all the wonderful things that many people in California are waiting to buy." She talked so fast that we didn't have a chance to answer. We just followed her. Neither Carmen nor I wanted to be alone in this dark place!

We hurried past a huge wooden tank that Mrs. Captain pointed out to us. She said the tank held all the ship's drinking water and that every day someone filled the much smaller red barrel with water from this huge tank. I remembered that red barrel! It was on deck next to the galley and it had caused me a lot of trouble! At the far end of the hold was a large storeroom. In the storeroom I saw hundreds of wooden barrels. "These barrels are filled with tea, clocks, ladies' paper fans, china dishes, ivory carvings, spyglasses, and small sewing tables," said Mrs. Captain.

I couldn't believe how many things were in the room. Each barrel was marked with large black letters.

"Where did you get all of these things?" I asked.

Mrs. Captain set the flickering lantern down on the top of a barrel. "Clara, do you remember seeing a long piece of paper that hung on the door when we entered the room?" I nodded. "That is the ship's cargo list. It lists everything that is in this room. The letters and markings on the barrels tell what is inside each one. The markings also tell where we bought or traded for the goods."

Mrs. Captain reached into a partly opened barrel and pulled out a small concertina. Brushing the packing straw away from it, she handed it to Carmen. Carmen was very excited. She said she would use it when she sang. Carmen pushed the concertina back and forth until the folds in the center filled with air. It made a squeaky noise.

Carmen's fingers played the buttons on the side of the concertina as someone would play the keys on the piano. At the same time, she pushed the concertina in and out. Like magic, music filled the room. Carmen was so pleased with her new treasure that she gave Mrs. Captain a huge hug.

Mrs. Captain picked up her lantern and motioned for us to follow her. As we walked behind her down the narrow passage, something furry jumped out from behind a barrel and brushed against my leg. I yelled and climbed onto a nearby crate.

"Walk the plank! Walk the plank!" screeched Blackbeard. Mrs. Captain smiled and calmly said, "It's just a rat, Clara. It is probably as afraid of you as you are of it!"

Mrs. Captain stopped near a large barrel. With a small jack knife that she kept in her pocket, she pried open the lid. She reached deep down into the straw and presented me with a wooden box. "This is a game called mah-jongg. It is for you, Clara." When I opened the box, I saw rectangular pieces of ivory. The ivory pieces were painted with trees and dragons.

"Mah-Jongg is an ancient Chinese game," said Mrs. Captain. "Sam-Lee has his own set and has taught many of the sailors on board to play."

At dinner I showed the mah-jongg game to

Sam-Lee. He said, "You are lucky to have such a most-honored game. The game mah-jongg has been played in China for more than two thousand years. Someday I will show you how to play mah-jongg."

Just as we finished dinner, Asa appeared in the galley with guess who? Murphy! "I found him sleeping on my bunk," Asa said. "Now how did that cat get into my cabin? He does get around doesn't he, Clara?" Laying Murphy in my lap, Asa looked at me and said, "Murphy's ship-wandering days will soon be over. In a few weeks, Clara, we will be arriving in California and you and your family will be leaving the ship."

Chapter Twenty-One

California At Last!

December 15, 1845
Monterey Bay, California

Boom! Boom! Boom! The cannon on board our ship thundered the news of the *Lady Shellhorn's* arrival in Monterey, the grand capital of Alta California.

Boom! Boom! Boom! was the reply from shore.

Mother, Father, and I stood on deck as our ship slowly sailed into the large, beautiful bay of Monterey. Gray and white seagulls greeted the ship with loud cries. A long, low-lying spit of land jutted out into the water. Waves crashed against the rocky cliffs sending white foam in all directions. Rays of sunlight slipped out from behind the gray clouds and I could see a few buildings on shore.

"Clara, would you like to use my spyglass to take a look at your new homeland?" Captain Nickels handed me his spyglass. I pressed the glass to my eye. I could see the fort and custom house and several other small buildings nestled among the sand dunes. Trees with tall trunks covered the cliffs and foothills.

*Looking up at the ship, I saw that everyone was standing by the
rail of the Lady Shellhorn waving their hats.*

"Do you see all the pine trees, Clara? Long ago the first explorers called this the Bay of Pines. The strong trunks of the pine trees are used as masts on many sailing ships."

Before long the *Lady Shellhorn* anchored two cable-lengths from shore. The sailors loaded our baggage into the ship's boat and I put Murphy into his basket.

All the sailors were dressed in their going-ashore clothes. They wore long white trousers, checkered shirts, and shiny black hats. They lined up to shake hands with us and say their good-byes.

I looked at all of our friends. After four months together, it was hard to leave everyone.

Mr. Turk tipped his hat and blew me a kiss. I know I saw tears in Mr. Simon's eyes as he looked at me over the top of his tiny glasses. Carmen and José talked excitedly in Spanish. The only word I understood was "adios." Mrs. Captain hugged me tightly while Blackbeard screeched, "Walk the plank! Walk the plank!"

All this time Asa stood quietly next to me. When Mrs. Captain stepped aside to talk to my parents, Asa bent down and whispered in my ear.

"Thank you, Clara, for being my friend and thank you for saving my life. I'll always remember you and your silly little cat, Murphy."

Next to say good-bye was dear Sam-Lee. He handed my mother a large basket filled with biscuits and then he turned to me.

"Clara, you are my special friend. Someday I will see you again and I will teach you how to play mah-jongg as I promised."

Sam-Lee stepped aside. Captain Nickels took my hand and shook it hard.

"Young lady, it will be mighty difficult to manage this ship without your help. When you're older, you will make a great sea captain."

My throat tightened and my eyes filled with tears. Captain Nickels continued talking to me.

"Don't be sad, Clara. Here's something from Mrs. Captain and me that you will be able to use when you're on the rancho. It will help you keep an eye on things. If you use it near the ocean who knows what you'll see? You may even see the *Lady Shellhorn!*"

From his coat pocket he took out a narrow box. He handed the box to me. I opened it. There was a shiny new silver spyglass!

As I stood looking at Captain Nickels, Father put his arm around my shoulders.

"Come, Clara," he said. "It's time to go ashore and meet your Uncle Frank."

We climbed down the ladder to the ship's boat. Looking up at the ship I saw that everyone was standing by the rail of the *Lady Shellhorn* waving their hats. The entire crew cheered, "Hip-Hip Hooray, Hip-Hip Hooray, Hip-Hip Hooray for Clara!"

Waving good-bye to everyone, I knew I'd never forget the brave shipmates who had brought us safely from Boston, round Cape Horn, to California!

Production services and printing by
Norco Billings Printing, San Leandro, CA 94577

Bibliography

Arlen, Karen, et al., **They Came Singing, Songs from California's History**. Oakland, CA: Calicanto Associates, 1995.

Bancroft, Hubert Howe. **History of California**. Volume III, 1825-1840. San Francisco, CA: The History Co., 1886.

Barker, Malcolm. **San Francisco Memoirs, 1835-1851.** San Francisco, CA: Londonborn Publications, 1994.

Carse, Robert.**The Moonrakers, The Story of the Clipper Ship Men**. New York, NY: Harper and Brothers, 1961.

Chichester, Francis. **Along the Clipper Way**. New York, NY: Coward McCann, Inc., 1966.

Cosgrave, John O'Hara. **Clipper Ship, America's Famous and Fast- Sailing Queens of the Sea**. New York, NY: The Macmillan Co., 1963.

Culver, Henry B. **The Book of Old Ships**. New York, NY: Dover Publications, 1992.

Dana, Richard Henry. **Two Years Before the Mast**. New York, NY: Airmont Publishing Co., Inc., 1965.

Delgado, James P. **To California by the Sea, A Maritime History of the California Gold Rush**. Columbia, SC: University of South Carolina Press, 1990.

De Pauw, Linda Grant. **Seafaring Women**. Boston, MA: Houghton Mifflin Co., 1982.

Fischer, Anton Otto. **Focs'le Days.** Kingston, NY: Hudson River Maritime Center, 1987.

Harlow, Frederick Pease. **The Making of a Sailor or Sea Life Aboard a Yankee Square-Rigger**. New York, NY: Dover Publications, 1988.

Johnson, Captain Irving. **The Peking Battles Cape Horn**. Peekskill, NY: Sea History Press, National Maritime Historical Society, 1995.

King, Dean, et al., **A Sea of Words**. New York, NY: Henry Holt and Co., 1995.

Knill, Henry. Editor. **Pirates**. Santa Barbara, CA: Bellerophon Books, 1975.

Lyon, Jane D. **Clipper Ships and Captains**. New York, NY: American Heritage Publishing Co., Inc., 1962.

Riesenberg, Felix. **Cape Horn**. Woodbridge, CT: Ox Bow Press, 1994.

Riesenberg, Felix. **Under Sail, A Boy's Voyage Around Cape Horn**. New York, NY: Harcourt, Brace Co., 1918.

Strong, Charles S. **The Story of American Sailing Ships**. New York, NY: Grosset and Dunlap, Inc., 1957.

Whipple, A.B.C.,et al., **The Clipper Ships**. Alexandria, Virginia: Time-Life Books, 1980.

Wollenberg, Charles. **Golden Gate Metropolis**. Berkeley, CA: Institute of Governmental Studies, University of California, 1985.

——————————. **Encyclopedia of Sailing**. New York, NY: Harper and Row, Publishers, 1971.

——————————-. **The Visual Encyclopedia of Nautical Terms Under Sail**. New York, NY: Crown Publishers, Inc., 1978.

Glossary

This glossary gives the meanings of words only as they are used in this book. You may wish to use a dictionary to find other meanings for these words.

accommodation ladder: a light staircase with handrails or ropes, fitted at the side of a ship for boarding

aft: at, near, or toward the back of a ship

ahoy: a call used by sailors to attract attention of persons at a distance

albatross: any of various large web-footed seabirds that can fly long distances; one of the largest seabirds

aloft: high above the deck of a ship; up among the sails, rigging, or masts of a ship

anchor: a shaped piece of iron attached to a chain or rope and used to hold a ship in place. The anchor grips the bottom and keeps the ship from drifting.

anchor short: the anchor chain is short when the chain is straight up and down in the water near the ship

Argentina: a country in South America; capital: Buenos Aires

aviary: a place where many birds are kept

ballast: heavy material such as stone placed low in a ship's hold to keep the ship stable

beam: a large long piece of timber

bilge pump: a pump used in sailing ships to draw up water from the lower part of the hull

binnacle box: a box containing a ship's compass, placed near the ship's wheel

boot trunk: a large box for holding boots or clothing, often attached to the back of a carriage or stagecoach

Boston: a seaport and capital of the state of Massachusetts

bosun: the officer responsible for the crew and for the ship's upkeep

bosun's chair: a chair that can be raised or lowered by ropes and pulleys. The chair can be used high in the mast or to lower someone over the side of a ship.

bow: the forward part of a ship

bowsprit: a pole projecting forward from the bow of a ship. Bowsprit is the main support of the foremast. Ropes from the bowsprit help to steady the sails and mast.

brace the yards: haul on the lines fastened to the outer ends of the yards to change the angle of the sails to make the best of the wind

brown pelican: see pelican

bulkhead: one of the walls dividing the ship into water-tight rooms to prevent leaking

cabin boy: a young seaman who sees to the needs of the officers

Cape Horn: an island off the very tip of South America

capstan: a machine for lifting or pulling; revolves on a shaft. Sailors push the long iron bars on the capstan to raise the anchor.

cargo: goods carried by a ship

Caribbean Sea: the sea between Central America, South America, and the West Indies

carriage: a vehicle on wheels usually pulled by horses and used to carry people

cast off: letting go the mooring lines and releasing the ropes that secure a ship to the dock

chant: a short, simple song that is sung over and over

Charlie Noble: the stovepipe in the galley of a ship

cleaver: a cutting tool with a heavy blade and a short handle

cobblestone: a rounded stone used as weight in the bottom of a ship. Cobblestones were used when there was no cargo to keep the ship stable.

cockroach: a small brown insect found anyplace in the world. Cockroaches are often found in kitchens and galleys.

coil: to wind around and around in a circular shape

companionway: a narrow stairway from the deck of a ship that leads down to the rooms below

compass: an instrument for showing directions

constellation: a group of stars such as The Big Dipper

continent: one of the seven great masses of land on the earth

Costa Rica: a country in Central America, north of Panama

crescent-shaped: shaped like a half circle

crow's nest: a seat or place high on the mast of a ship, used as a lookout

deck house: a small house on the top deck of the ship with small rooms for the galley, the sailmaker, the carpenter, and sometimes the captain's map room

Doldrums: region of the ocean near the equator where the wind is very light

Donkey's Breakfast: pieces of canvas sewn into the shape of a sack, filled with straw, and used as a mattress by sailors

duff: a seaman's pudding made of flour, molasses, and sometimes dried fruit and boiled in a cloth bag

embroider: to make a design on cloth with stitches using a needle and thread

emperor: a man who rules a large empire or country

eye-bolt: an iron bolt driven into the decks with an eye at one end to which ropes can be fastened

fore: at the front or toward the front of a ship

forecastle: the upper deck in front of the foremast that contains the sailors' quarters

fo'c'sl: see forecastle

funnel: a tapered tube with a wide cone-shaped mouth used to prevent spills when pouring a liquid into a container with a small opening

furl: to gather in a sail, rolling it up and tying it to the yard or mast.

galley: the kitchen on board a ship

gimbals: devices that hold something level. The compass bowl rests on gimbals that keep it level as the ship rolls and pitches.

hardtack: a very hard dry biscuit eaten by sailors

hatch: an opening in a ship's deck through which the cargo is loaded

haul: to pull or drag with force

hawser: a large rope used for towing or mooring ships

heave away: to lift with force and effort

helmsman: man who steers the ship

herb: a plant whose leaves or stems are used for medicine, seasoning food, or perfume

hoist: to raise or lift up often using ropes and pulleys

hold: the interior of a ship below the deck where a ship's cargo is carried

holystone: a piece of soft sandstone used for scrubbing the wooden deck of a ship

hull: the body or frame of the ship

humdrum: dull, without variety, no excitement

hurricane lamp: an oil lamp or candlestick with a tall glass chimney to keep the flame from being blown out

jib: the triangular sail at the front of the ship

Jolly Roger: a pirate's black flag with a skull and crossbones on it

lanyard: any short piece of line tied to an object to hold it steady

lash: to tie or fasten something with rope

lather: foam made from soap and water

lifeline: any rope attached to the ship to help the crew work during bad weather

lines: ropes used on board a ship for hoisting sails, towing, leading, and many other general purposes

lurch: a sudden leaning or roll to one side

mah-jongg: a game that began in China and is played with 144 domino-like pieces.

main hatch: see hatch

mast: a tall strong pole of

wood set upright on a ship to support the sails and rigging

megaphone: a large funnel-shaped horn used to make the voice louder

merchant: a person who buys and sells goods

musty: a smell like mold or moldy dampness

overhead: ceiling

papaya: a tropical American tree with large leaves and an edible melon-like fruit

passageway: a narrow hallway on a ship

Peking, China: capital of China for more than five centuries

pelican: a large fish-eating waterbird with a huge bill and a pouch on the underside of the bill

periwinkle: a low plant with blue flowers

pilot: a person who helps steer ships in or out of a harbor or through dangerous waters

port: a place where ships can be sheltered from a storm; a

harbor; the left side of the ship when facing the bow

porthole: an opening in a ship's side to let in light and air; a window

quarters: a certain part of the ship where people live or work, such as the captain's quarters

rancho: the Spanish word for ranch

rigging: ropes used to support and work the masts, yards, sails, etc. on a ship
  —**standing rigging:** ropes that support the masts and yards
  —**running rigging:** ropes used in working the sails

Rio de Janeiro: a large seaport in Brazil, South America

rudder: a hinged flat piece of wood at the stern of a ship by which it is steered

running rigging: see rigging

rustle: a soft, light sound of things gently rubbing together, such as the sound of leaves being moved by a gentle breeze
sail: a large piece of cloth, usually canvas, spread to face the wind to make a ship

move through the water

sailmaker: a person who makes or repairs sails

saltwater soap: a special soap that lathers or foams when used with salt water

scurry (scurried): to run quickly or hurry

sea legs: ability to walk without the loss of balance on board a ship, especially in a rough sea

shanty: a song sung by sailors in rhythm with the motions made during their work, such as pulling on ropes or heaving at the capstan

sheath knife: a knife carried in a case or covering to protect its blade; used when eating meals; carried as a safety measure when working in the rigging

skylight: a window in a roof or ceiling

slick: smooth; slippery; greasy

slop chest: a small room where extra clothing and supplies are kept and sold to the sailors on board a ship
　　—**slops:** extra clothing for

the crew of a ship

sou'wester (southwester): a waterproof hat having a broad brim behind to protect the neck, worn by seamen

spunk: having courage; spirit

spyglass: a small telescope

square-rigger: a sailing ship with main sails that are large and square

squawk: a loud, harsh sound

stagnate: to become foul or spoiled, especially water that does not run or flow such as swamp water or water that collects below the decks of a ship

stalk: the stem or main part of a plant that supports the branches and leaves

standing rigging: see rigging

starboard: the right side of a ship when facing forward

steer (steering): to direct or guide a ship by means of a rudder controlled by a wheel

stern: the hind or rear part of a ship

swell(s): a large, long unbroken wave or waves

tallow: the hard fat from sheep or cows used for making candles or soap

three-masted: a ship that has three masts to hold the sails, the foremast, main mast, and mizzen mast

tidbit: a very pleasing bit of food

tow: to pull another ship through the water by means of a rope or hawser

towboat: a boat used to pull another ship through the water by means of a rope or hawser

unfurl: to release or let down a sail that has been gathered and tied to the yard or mast

watch: to be on lookout or guard; a period of time that sailors spend on duty watching the ship and sea. Time at sea is divided into five, four-hour watches that run from 8PM in the evening to 4PM the next afternoon. There are two dogwatches, 4 to 6PM and 6 to 8PM in the evening.

weevil: a small beetle-like insect that destroys grains, fruit, cotton, etc.

whittle: to cut shavings or chips from a piece of wood with a knife; to shape a piece of wood by carving it

yard: a spar or pole mounted across a mast to carry sails

yardarm: either end of a long, slender beam or pole used to support a square sail

yarn: a story or tale usually told by a sailor

yerba buena: a sweet smelling herb found growing in the hills of the pueblo of San Francisco; an area that was a part of the pueblo of San Francisco called Yerba Buena